Little Duck's First Christmas

Some other books to enjoy:

Duck's Easter Egg Hunt
Written by Dawn Richards,
illustrated by Heidi D'hamers

Mole's Harvest Moon
Mouse's Christmas Wish
By Judi Abbot

LITTLE DUCK'S FIRST CHRISTMAS
A PICTURE CORGI BOOK
978 0 552 56668 1
First published in Great Britain by Picture Corgi,
an imprint of Random House Children's Publishers UK
A Random House Group Company
This edition published 2012
9 7 5 3 1 2 4 6 8 10
Text copyright © Random House Children's Publishers UK, 2012 Illustrations copyright © Heidi D'hamers, 2012
The right of Heidi D'hamers to be identified as the illustrator of this work has been asserted in accordance with the Copyright, Designs and Patents Act 1988.
Picture Corgi Books are published by Random House Children's Publishers UK, 61–63 Uxbridge Road, London W5 5SA
www.kidsatrandomhouse.co.uk
www.randomhouse.co.uk
Addresses for companies within The Random House Group Limited can be found at:
www.randomhouse.co.uk/offices.htm
THE RANDOM HOUSE GROUP Limited Reg. No. 954009
A CIP catalogue record for this book is available from the British Library.
Printed in China

Little Duck's First Christmas

Dawn Richards & Heidi D'hamers

Picture Corgi

It was the day before Christmas. Snow was falling gently in the village, as everyone helped with the final preparations.

The Hedgehog family had made some mince pies.

The Mole family sang Christmas carols.

The Cat and Rabbit families were decorating
the huge Christmas tree.

And the Duck family . . .

Well, the Duck family felt particularly excited –
it was Little Duck's first ever Christmas.

"Will the Christmas Bear come and give me lots of presents?"
Little Duck asked anxiously.

"Of course," quacked Mummy Duck with a smile. "You've
been a very good little duck all year, so don't you worry."

But Little Duck did worry. "Am I really a good little duck?" she wondered. "Am I good enough for the Christmas Bear to come?" She couldn't think of one very good thing that she'd done.

"I know something really good I can do," said Little Duck
to herself.

"I'll go to the Christmas market and get Mummy and
Daddy a special present to open on Christmas morning."

Pleased with her good idea, Little Duck wrapped herself up warmly and set off for the Christmas market. It was open all day, so she would have lots of time to choose the perfect gift.

But as she was walking along the road - **WHOMP!**
Little Duck felt something cold hit her on the back.
"Ooof!" said Little Duck. "What was that?"

"Gotcha," said Caspar Cat, and he bent down to pick up another snowball. Little Duck was about to get cross, when she saw a snowball flying towards Casper Cat.

WHACK went the snowball as it landed right on his head. "Ha ha!" laughed Mary Mole. Casper did look funny.

Soon Little Duck was deep in the middle of a snowball fight with her friends.

"Now let's build a snow mountain," called Mary.

"That is a really **good** snow mountain," said Casper, feeling satisfied.

"**Good!**" thought Little Duck, suddenly remembering.

"I'm not being a **good** little duck at all – the Christmas Bear will never come!" and with that she hurried on towards the market.

As Little Duck waddled on her way, she suddenly heard a . . .

WHOOOOSH! WHIZZZ! "Weeeeeeeee!"

What could it be?

It was her friends Harry Hedgehog and Ben Badger.
"Come and have a go on our sled," they cried.

Soon Little Duck was whizzing down the hill.

"This hill's all right," said Ben Badger. "But I know a really **good** hill for sledding."
"**Good!**" thought Little Duck as she remembered her plan.

"I'm not being a **good** little duck at all – the Christmas Bear will never come!" And she left her friends and sped on towards the market.

But as she hurried along she stumbled across Sammy Goose.
"What are you doing lying in the snow?" asked Little Duck.
"I'm making snow angels," said Sammy Goose. "It's fun!"

So Little Duck helped Sammy Goose make shapes in the snow.
"Look," said Sammy breathlessly. "We've made ten **good**
little angels."

"**Good!**" thought Little Duck – she had forgotten again . . .
"I'm being a very **bad** little duck – the Christmas Bear will
never come!"

And she quickly brushed herself down and rushed on
towards the market.

Closed

But when Little Duck reached the Christmas market, it had already closed.

Oh no, Little Duck!

Little Duck walked home sadly along the snowy path and past the frozen lake. By the lake she saw Dog, busy making beautiful ice sculptures.

When Little Duck explained what had happened, Dog gave her a lovely little ice duck. The perfect gift for Mummy and Daddy Duck.

Little Duck carefully put the ice duck in her pocket and then hurried home, as it was getting very late.
"Where have you been?" quacked Mummy and Daddy Duck when Little Duck arrived home. "We were so worried."

"I've been a very good little duck. And I have a surprise for you."

But when Little Duck reached into her pocket to put the ice
duck under the tree, all she found was a puddle of water.
The little ice duck had melted all away.

Little Duck was miserable. She crept into bed and sobbed quietly to herself. The Christmas Bear would never come, and neither she nor her parents would have any presents on Christmas morning.

Finally Little Duck fell asleep, but in the middle of the night she awoke to a strange sound. She crept down to the living room to see what it could be . . .

It was the **Christmas Bear!**

"But I haven't been good," whispered Little Duck.
"You've had a very good try," laughed the Christmas Bear,
"and that's what counts."

The room was full of magic as the Christmas Bear placed present after present under the tree.

"Now, don't open them until morning," he said with a wink.
Then, with a shimmer of magic, he disappeared.

The next morning, Little Duck opened her presents in a flutter and a flap of excitement. She had lots of toys and sweets from the Christmas Bear and some special treats from her mum and dad.

"But I don't have a present for you," said Little Duck sadly.
"Oh, we don't need a present," said Mummy and Daddy Duck,
giving each other a big smile.

"And maybe we can help play
with your presents," laughed
Daddy Duck.

Later that morning the Duck family went out into the village to say Merry Christmas to all their friends.

"What did you get for Christmas?" Cat asked Mummy Duck.

"We shared a wonderful Christmas cuddle," said Mummy Duck.

The best present of all!